SPACE HOPPERS

MUDMEN OF MARS

TOMMY DONBAVAND

NASEN House, 4/5 Amber Business Village, Amber Close, Amington, Tamworth, Staffordshire, B77 4RP

Rising Stars UK Ltd.
7 Hatchers Mews, Bermondsey Street, London SE1 3GS
www.risingstars-uk.com

Text and design © Rising Stars UK Ltd.
The right of Tommy Donbavand to be identified as the author of this work has been asserted by him in accordance with the Copyright, Design and Patents Act, 1998.

Published 2014

Author: Tommy Donbavand
Cover design: Sarah Garbett @ Sg Creative Services
Illustrations: Alan Brown for Advocate Art
Text design and typesetting: Sarah Garbett @ Sg Creative Services
Publisher: Fiona Lazenby
Editorial consultants: Jane Friswell and Dee Reid
Editorial: Fiona Tomlinson and Sarah Chappelow

All rights reserved. No part of this publication may be reproduced, stored in a retrieval system or transmitted in any form by any means, electronic, mechanical, photocopying, recording or otherwise without the prior permission of Rising Stars.

British Library Cataloguing in Publication Data.
A CIP record of this book is available from the British Library.

ISBN: 978-1-78339-322-0

Printed in the UK by Ashford Colour Press Ltd, Gosport, Hampshire

CONTENTS

Name: Dan Fireball
Rank: Captain
Age: 12
Home planet: Earth
Most likely to: hide behind the Captain's chair and ask timidly, "Are we there yet?"

Name: Astra Moon
Rank: Second Officer
Age: 11
Home planet: The Moon
Most likely to: face up to The Geezer, strike a karate pose and say, "Bring it on!"

HS INFINITY

THE GEEZER

VOLT

Name: Volt
Rank: Agent
Age: Really old!
Home planet: Venus
Most likely to: puff steam from his shoulder exhausts and announce, "Hop completed!"

GUS

Name: Gus Buster
Rank: Head of COSMIC
Age: 15
Home planet: Earth
Most likely to: suddenly appear on the view screen and yell, "Fireball, where are you?"

VOLT

Greetings new recruits!

My name is Volt and I shall be your cyber-teacher for today.

You should read this section because if you wish to become **COSMIC** agents you must know the history of the Solar System.

Long ago, adults used to be in charge of everything. They had jobs, ran governments and were in charge of television remote controls.

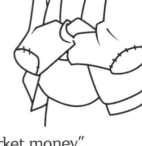

Children were forced to stay in school until the age of 18. They had to do everything their parents told them. They were only given small amounts of currency, known as "pocket money".

There were lots of problems. Adults polluted the Earth and then went on to do the same — or even worse — on the remaining eight planets of our Solar System. In fact, for a long time, adults even refused to call Pluto a real planet!

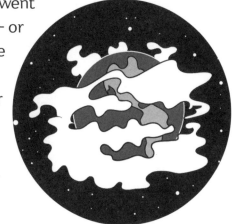

So, in the year 2281, the children took over.

Adults were made to retire at the age of 18 and were sent to retirement homes on satellites in space. Children just needed three years at school, so most children were working by the time they were eight years old.

The Solar System quickly became a much happier, safer and cleaner place to live.

However, not all of the adults liked having to retire at the age of 18. Some of them rebelled and escaped from their retirement homes on satellites in

space. They began to cause trouble and commit crimes.

That's why **COSMIC** was created:

Crimes
   Of
      Serious
         Magnitude
            Investigation
               Company

The worst of these villains was known as The Geezer. The purpose of COSMIC was to stop The Geezer from committing crimes.

Members of COSMIC flew around the Solar System solving mysteries and bringing badly behaved adults to justice. The COSMIC spaceships could navigate an invisible series of magnetic tunnels called the Hop Field, so they were called Space Hoppers.

I myself, was a member of one such team of Space Hoppers, alongside the famous agents - Dan Fireball and Astra Moon.

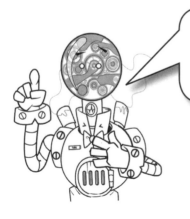

If you turn the page, you can read about the first mission we ever undertook in our Hop Ship, the HS Infinity ...

 CHAPTER 1

LOOKING GOOD

HS INFINITY DATA LOG
MISSION REPORT 1:
MUDMEN OF MARS
REPORT BEGINS ...

Captain Dan Fireball sat in his chair on the command deck of the HS Infinity and stared silently at the huge view screen in front of

him. On it he could see the Earth below and, beyond that, millions of miles of black, empty space.

At her own desk on a raised platform behind the Captain's chair, Second Officer Astra Moon tapped a series of calculations into her computer and said, "We're ready to enter the Hop Field, Captain."

Captain Fireball didn't reply. Astra tried again. "Captain…?"

Still nothing.

"Dan! Wake up!" Astra threw her pen at the back of the Captain's head.

Dan jumped up and rubbed at the spot where the pen had hit him. "Ow!" he cried. "What did you do that for?"

"You were staring at yourself in the view screen again," said Astra.

"I was not!" said Dan. "I was … studying the miles of empty space."

Astra giggled. "The only empty space around here is the one between your ears."

Dan tried to look cross, but failed. "You're not supposed to talk to me like that now I'm the Captain," he laughed.

Astra folded her arms. "We both scored exactly the same number of points on the exam," she reminded him. "The only reason COSMIC made you the Captain instead of me is because you come from a rich and powerful family."

"That's not true!" said Dan. "I'm a perfectly normal 12-year-old."

"Who likes to stare at himself in his new uniform," added Astra.

Dan smoothed down the front of his sleek, red jumpsuit and grinned. "I do look rather smart, don't I?

I always imagined this is how I would look when I finally became the Captain of my own Hop Ship."

Just then the doors to the command deck hissed open and an old, brass robot rolled in on a single wheel. Sparks fizzed between the robot's eyes, and steam pumped from twin exhaust pipes behind its shoulders.

"I'm sorry to interrupt," said Volt. "But we have an urgent message coming in from COSMIC headquarters."

Dan sat back in the Captain's chair. "Put it on the screen."

Volt tapped a command into his computer keyboard and the image on the screen changed to 15-year-old boy. He leaned in towards the camera, filling the screen with his serious round face. It was Chief Gus Buster, the head of COSMIC.

"Chief!" said Dan, giving a smart salute. "Good to see you. How are things back at HQ? Still delighted with your choice for Captain of this ship, I hope?"

Astra sighed.

"No time to chat, Fireball," growled The Chief. "I know this is your first day in charge of the HS Infinity, but we've got an emergency and yours is the only Hop Ship available."

"We're ready to leave whenever you give the command, Chief," said Astra.

The Chief nodded. "I'm uploading the space map reference for your destination to you now, Astra," he said.

"Got it," said Astra as the co-ordinates appeared on her computer display.

"Good luck everyone," said The Chief as his face disappeared from the screen.

"Hurry up Astra," said Dan. "We need to set off."

"Just double checking the calculations," said Astra. "You won't look as good in your uniform if we jump into the Hop Field and leave half your atoms behind here."

Dan looked shocked. "Take your time, then," he said. "I don't want any mistakes!"

"Okay," said Astra a moment later. "Let's Hop!" She slammed her palm down on to a large yellow button on the console in front of her. The HS Infinity leapt sideways into one of the invisible magnetic tunnels that make up the Hop Field, connecting every planet and moon in the Solar System. Within seconds, the ship was whizzing along.

For a moment everything went fuzzy - as though the entire universe was made out of candy floss. Astra clung on to the edge of her desk. Her mouth was dry, and it felt like someone was tickling her all over.

The view screen at the front of the ship crackled. The image of the Earth flickered slightly, and then vanished. Hissing static appeared for a moment and then, with a pop, the screen settled to reveal that they were now in orbit over a massive, red world.

"Hop completed," said Volt, calmly.

"What should we do now?" asked Astra, turning to the Captain's chair.

But Captain Dan Fireball wasn't sitting in his chair any longer. He was crouched down behind it, his normally perfect hair standing on end like a dandelion.

He rose shakily to his feet. "Are we there yet?" he croaked.

Astra tried her best to hide her smile. "Yes Captain," she said. "We've arrived safely. We're in orbit above the planet Mars."

CHAPTER 2

DUST TO DUST

The door to the HS Infinity slid open, Dan and Astra stepped out on to a new world. They both wore glass helmets attached to the collars of their uniforms. Volt wheeled out, closing the door behind them.

The ship had come to rest near the edge of a deep valley.

"Nice landing!" said Dan.

Astra smiled. "A little bumpy for my liking, but I'll get used to it."

They looked at the landscape stretching out in front of them. All they could see, in every direction, was a vast red desert, dotted with crimson stones and big rocks.

Dan rubbed his boot in the red dust at his feet. "You know, years ago, some people believed that aliens from Mars were planning to invade the Earth," he said.

"I read about that," said Astra. "Then it turned out that Martians were the most peaceful people in the entire Solar System."

Dan looked around. "The question is: where are all these peaceful Martians?"

Astra looked at the Captain in surprise. "It's summer on Mars at the moment," she pointed out. "The Martians will all be in hibernation. Surely you remember that from our training?"

"Of course I do," Dan lied. "But where? All I can see is dust!"

Astra turned to Volt. "You tell him."

"Of course, Miss Astra," said the robot. "Master Dan - the Martians are the dust."

Dan stopped rubbing his boot in the red dirt. "Really?"

"Yes, really!" said Astra. "I knew you hadn't paid attention in our lesson about Mars."

Volt continued. "At hotter times of the year, Martians dry out and hibernate as dust to avoid losing precious water. Then, when the weather is cooler, they can be rehydrated."

"Ah yes. I remember now," said Dan. "But, then who called COSMIC for help?"

"My sensors indicate the emergency call came from a position near to that large pile of rocks," said Volt, wheeling away. Dan and Astra followed the robot to a small mound of red earth at the foot of a rocky hill.

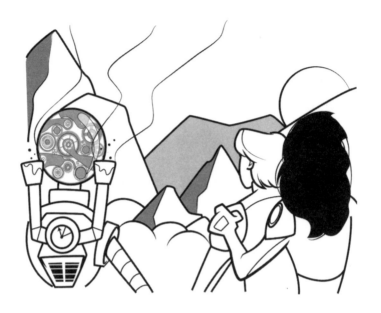

"Leave this to me," said Dan. He crouched down and spoke loudly to the pile of dust. "Er ... hello? This is Captain Dan Fireball of the HS Infinity. We are responding to your request for help."

After a moment of silence, Dan stood up again. "He's not talking."

Astra produced a bottle of water from her backpack. "You'll need this," she said.

"No, thanks," said Dan. "I had a cup of tea just before we set off."

"It's not for you," sighed Astra. "It's to rehydrate our Martian friend. Watch!"

Dan stepped back and watched as Astra poured the bottle of water over the mound of dust. Instantly, the crimson powder began to fizz and bubble. It grew taller, sprouting arms and a head.

FIZZZZ!

In less than a minute, what appeared to be a snowman made out of red mud was standing in front of them.

The creature blinked in the sunlight, then reached out and grabbed Dan by the hand. "Oh, thank goodness you've come," it gurgled wetly. "I'm Edgar. We need your help!"

Dan pulled his hand free and stared at the lumps of red mud sticking to his glove. "And I need a wet wipe!" he said.

Astra pulled out her handheld computer and made some notes. "Okay, Edgar," she said. "What's the problem?"

"It's my nephew," said Edgar. "He's been kidnapped."

"Was he ... a Mudman, like you?" asked Dan.

Edgar shook his head. "He was taken mid-hibernation. He's still dust!"

"Okay," said Astra, jotting down the information. "And what is your nephew's name?"

"Dusty," said Edgar.

"Of course it is," mumbled Dan. "But, how can you tell he's been kidnapped?"

"Isn't it obvious?" replied Edgar. "Look ..."

The Mudman pointed to an area of red dust that Dan and Astra thought looked just like any other.

"Please allow me to inspect the crime scene," said Volt, rolling into position. Lenses appeared from a slot in Volt's body, allowing him to zoom in on the evidence at hand.

"Well?" said Dan. "Can you see anything?"

"I'm afraid so, Captain," said Volt. "Mr Edgar is correct; it would appear that a portion of the ground has indeed been scooped up and removed."

"Who would do such a thing?" said Astra.

With a hiss, Volt raised his head up from his shoulders on a long, brass pole.

It turned in a complete circle, then lowered back down again. "I suspect you will find the answer to that question on the other side of these rocks."

Dan and Astra looked at each other, then scrambled up to the top of the mini-mountain. On the other side was a deep canyon, in the middle of which sat a small house, surrounded by a white wooden fence.

CHAPTER 3

SHADY ACRES

A stra pulled a pair of binoculars from her backpack and stared at the house through them.

It had a flower garden at the front, and the windows were decorated with lace curtains. "Who would build a house in the middle of nowhere on Mars?" she asked.

Dan took the binoculars to study the building himself. "That's not a house," he said. "That's a spaceship. It's one of those retirement homes for adults. My Dad's company helped to design them before he retired."

"But, retirement homes are not supposed to land," said Astra. "They were built to remain in orbit around the Earth."

"If I remember correctly," said Dan, "one of the retirement homes - Shady Acres - was hijacked and modified by a criminal adult called The Geezer. I think this could be that ship."

"The Geezer!" said Astra with a gasp. "He's one of the most wanted criminals in the entire Solar System."

"Correction, Miss Astra," said Volt. "He is currently *the* most wanted criminal."

"And you think The Geezer is the one scooping up dust from Mars?" asked Edgar.

Dan lowered his binoculars. "There's only one way to find out ..."

It took the team almost an hour to reach the house at the bottom of the canyon. Volt extended a skeleton key from one of his hands and picked the lock.

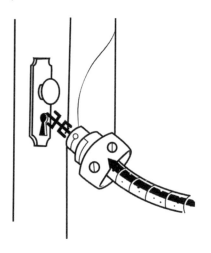

Within seconds the Space Hoppers and Edgar were creeping through the dark kitchen of the house.

"So, what do we do if we bump into The Geezer in here?" whispered Astra.

Dan froze. "I hadn't thought that far ahead," he admitted.

"The Geezer is wanted on Earth for several crimes," said Volt. "A Hop Ship Captain would be required to arrest him and return him for trial."

"A Hop Ship Captain ..." muttered Dan. "You mean me, don't you?"

Volt bowed slightly on his single wheel. "I do indeed, sir!"

Dan turned to Astra. "It's not too late for you to challenge the Chief's decision to make me the Captain, you know."

Astra nudged him on. "Just keep moving." she hissed. "We'll deal with The Geezer as a team - if and when we find him."

Dan, Astra and Volt went into a comfortable sitting room, also in darkness. High-backed armchairs lined every wall. It took Astra a moment before she realised that there were people sitting silent and unmoving in them.

"Look!" she hissed, producing a torch and shining a weak beam of light around the room. "There are people here! Old people."

"*Really* old people!" said Dan, pulling a face. "They must be in their thirties, at least!"

"They've all got some kind of red goo covering their faces," said Astra.

"That's not goo!" cried Edgar. "That's Martian mud! Bits of my friends and family!"

Suddenly, bright lights came on and the crew found themselves faced with a figure, standing in the doorway. He wore a grey knitted cardigan, brown trousers and comfy slippers.

"The Geezer!" snarled Dan.

"The very same," replied the criminal. "But, I'm afraid I do not know who you are."

Dan stood on the spot for a second shaking with fear. Then he turned to Astra.

"I've forgotten my name!" he squeaked.

Astra rolled her eyes. "We are a COSMIC Space Hopper crew from Earth," she announced. "I am Second Officer Astra Moon, and this is Captain Dan Fireball!"

The Geezer's eyes grew wide, and he stepped into the room. "Fireball?" he said "*The* Dan Fireball?"

Dan nodded, trembling. "You've heard of me?"

"Not exactly," The Geezer smiled. "But I know your father!"

"You know Darius Fireball?" said Astra.

"Yes," said The Geezer. "Or, at least, I knew him before you pesky children forced adults into retirement against our will."

"But, adults enjoy early retirement," said Astra.

"Is that what they're teaching you back at COSMIC?" said The Geezer. "Take a look around you, children. Do these people look happy to you?"

"They look dirty," said Dan. "Why have you slapped mud all over their faces?"

"It's not just any old mud," smiled The Geezer. "They're mudpacks. My own recipe - designed especially to make my customers younger!"

"He is correct," said Volt. "In the time we have been here, these adults have reversed in age by nine months."

"A beauty product that really reverses ageing," beamed The Geezer. "Before long, they will be young enough to legally come back out of retirement, and then we old folks will re-take control of the Solar System!"

"No, you won't!" gurgled Edgar. "You are using Martian dust, the mush and mud of living Mudmen, to make your face packs. We will not allow this to continue!"

"We do use dust from this lonely planet," admitted The Geezer. "But then, of course, there is my secret ingredient."

"What is it?" demanded Dan. "What is this secret ingredient?"

The Geezer sighed. "If I told you, it wouldn't be a secret, would it?" He turned to Astra. "Did COSMIC really make him a Captain?"

Volt's eyes flashed, "My scanners indicate a large tank of liquid in the next room."

"The secret ingredient, no doubt!" said Astra. "Place The Geezer under arrest while the Captain and I investigate."

"Yes, Miss Astra!" Volt wheeled over to The Geezer and grabbed one of the man's wrists with his robotic hand. His eyes flashed, "You're nicked, Grandad!"

Dan and Astra pulled open the door to the next room. On the other side, they found themselves in the massive engine room of the ship. At the back of the room one end was a skip filled to brim with red dust and, at the other, stood a huge glass tank marked 'Kitten Tears'.

CHAPTER 4

GLORIOUS MUD

"The secret ingredient is kitten tears?" cried Astra.

Dan stared up at the huge container. "How did he get that many kittens to cry?"

Astra shook her head. "I don't want to know."

"Dusty!" exclaimed Edgar. He slid over to the skip full of Martian soil and scooped a handful out.

"That's him?" said Dan. "That's your nephew?"

Edgar nodded. "I'd know him anywhere."

Astra produced the water bottle from her belt. "Put him on the floor." Edgar placed the dust in a little mound and Astra tipped out what was left of her water on top of it. The dirt began to twist and shift, then a smaller, younger Mudman grew up out of it.

"Uncle Edgar!" he cried, throwing muddy arms around the older Martian. "I knew you'd come to rescue me."

"Are you Okay?" Edgar asked, looking his nephew up and down.

"I am now," said Dusty. "But they've got hundreds of others in there." He pointed at the skip. "Aunt Freda, cousin Hal, that guy who runs holiday trips to Phobos ..."

"Don't worry," said Astra. "Once we've transported The Geezer back to Earth, we'll return all your friends to their hibernation spots."

"I'm afraid that won't be possible," said a voice. Dan and Astra spun round to find The Geezer entering the room. "My mudpack plan will continue uninterrupted."

"Where's Volt?" said Astra angrily.

The Geezer smiled. "My youthful assistants are looking after him," he said. "And they are about to do the same for you." He clicked his fingers and a dozen adults with mud packs on their faces strode into the room. They grabbed Astra, Dan, Edgar and Dusty by the arms and held them firm.

"You won't get away with this!" barked Dan.

"And who's going to stop me?" said The Geezer. "Not Captain Dan Fireball or his faithful sidekick, Astra Moon, that's for certain. A handful of mudpack treatments each and you'll both be helpless babies again." He scooped a handful of red dust from the skip and laughed. "In fact, let's start right now."

"That won't be happening, old man," said Dan. "You see, I've only just been given this Captain's uniform. It fits perfectly, and it's going to stay that way." Then he jumped forward and blew the dust into The Geezer's face.

The Geezer stumbled backwards, choking and spluttering. "Water!" he spat. "I need water." He fell against a control panel and knocked a large lever.

Suddenly, the tank marked 'Kitten Tears' began to rumble. Everyone watched in horror the tank split open and millions of gallons of salty liquid poured out into the room and ran down the ship's drains.

"Uh-oh!" said Astra. "I think we'd better get out of here."

"Leave that to us!" said Edgar. He and Dusty dropped to the floor as puddles of red gunge, escaping from their captors. Then they instantly reformed and grabbed hold of the adults clutching Dan and Astra.

"Go!" yelled Edgar. "Now!"

Dan and Astra rescued Volt from the next room, then they all raced out of the back door. The ground around the ship was flooded as the kitten tears continued to pour out of the ship's drainage system, and they found themselves struggling through the sticky mud.

Then the mud began to bubble, and twist, and grow.

Dan, Astra and Volt threw themselves clear, just as a Martian Mudman the size of a skyscraper rose up from the red soil. Towering over the retirement home spaceship, the mud monster threw back its head and roared.

"Powerful stuff, those kitten tears!" shouted Dan over the noise.

They watched as the massive Mudman picked up the house in a gloopy hand. Edgar and Dusty appeared at one of the windows, pushing the skip of red dust. They tipped it out on to the planet below.

"JUMP!" shouted Astra.

Dusty and Edgar leapt from the window and landed on the Mudman's shoulder, just as the creature swung its arm and hurled Shady Acres Retirement Home out into deep space. Astra could just hear the furious scream of The Geezer as he was hurled through Mars' atmosphere and into black empty space.

Its task completed, the mud monster sank back down into the ground and disappeared.

Dan stood up and tried to wipe some of the squelchy red mud from his sleek Captain's uniform. The stuff was matted into his hair, filled his boots, and he even had a couple of lumps stuck up his nose.

"I looked so good in the view screen this morning," he sighed.

Astra laughed. "The sun will dry us out," she said. "And we'll be a lot dirtier after we've finished helping Edgar and Dusty return everyone to their hibernation spots."

Volt rolled over to them, his wheel slipping and skidding in the mud. "We failed in our mission. We should have arrested The Geezer for his crimes," he pointed out.

Astra glanced up at the sky. There was no sign of Shady Acres Retirement Home. "Do you think we'll come across him again?" she asked.

Dan pulled his hand free of the gluey goo and ran his fingers through his messy hair. "Almost certainly," he said. "In fact, I've got a horrible feeling that we're going to be stuck with him for some time to come."

THE END

Now read *Silence on Saturn* to find out what The Geezer gets up to next!

GLOSSARY

atmosphere — the gases that are all around a planet

binoculars — special lenses that you look through with both eyes to make far away things look closer

calculation — ways of working things out using maths

co-ordinates — a pair of numbers that are used to find something on a map or grid

hibernation — a long sleep used to save energy. Some animals on Earth hibernate through the winter.

Martian — creatures that live on the planet Mars

modified — changed in some way

rehydrated — something that has had water put back into it

QUIZ QUESTIONS

1   Which of Dan and Astra scored highest in their exam?

2   What is the name of the Chief?

3   What is Edgar's nephew's name?

4   How was Volt able to see over the mound of rocks?

5   What is the name of the criminal adult who hijacked the retirement ship?

6   How did the Space Hoppers get inside the house?

7   Why is The Geezer taking the Martian mud?

8   What are the names of Edgar's other Martian relations who have been put into the skip?

9   What threw the retirement ship back into space?

10 Why does Dan say: "I looked so good in the view screen this morning."?

ABOUT THE AUTHOR

Tommy Donbavand writes full-time and lives in Lancashire with his family. He is also the author of the 13-book *Scream Street* series (currently in production for TV) and has written numerous books for children and young adults.

For Tommy, the best thing about being an author is getting to spend his days making up adventures for his readers. He also writes for 'The Bash Street Kids' in *The Beano*, which excites him beyond belief!

Find out more about Tommy and his other books at www.tommydonbavand.com

QUIZ ANSWERS

1   They scored the same.
2   Chief Gus Buster
3   Dusty
4   He raised his head up from his shoulders on a long, brass pole.
5   The Geezer
6   Volt had a skeleton key and picked the lock.
7   To create a beauty product that reverses ageing.
8   Aunt Freda and cousin Hal
9   A giant Martian Mudman
10 Because now he is all covered in squelchy red mud.